I Am Tama, Lucky Cat

A Japanese
Legend

12/11
16.95

To my mother and in memory of my father,

parents who always said yes to strays brought home

—W. H.

To Fuka and Taiki

—Y. J.

Published by
PEACHTREE PUBLISHERS
1700 Chattahoochee Avenue
Atlanta, Georgia 30318-2112
www.peachtree-online.com

Text ©2011 by Wendy Henrichs
Illustrations ©2011 by Yoshiko Jaeggi
Photographs, page 32 ©2011 by Barbara and Jerry Conner

Art direction by Loraine M. Joyner
Illustrations created in watercolor on archival 100% rag
watercolor paper. Title and text typeset in Bernd Montag's
Chantelli Antiqua.

Printed in March 2011 by Tien Wah Press in Singapore
10 9 8 7 6 5 4 3 2 1
First Edition

Library of Congress Cataloging-in-Publication Data

Henrichs, Wendy.
   I am Tama, lucky cat / written by Wendy Henrichs; illustrated
by Yoshiko Jaeggi.
      p. cm.
   Summary: A retelling of the traditional Japanese tale describing
the origins of the beckoning cat and how it came to be a symbol
of good luck.
   ISBN 978-1-56145-589-8 / 1-56145-589-X
   [1. Folklore--Japan. 2. Cats--Folklore.] I. Jaeggi, Yoshiko, ill. II.
Title.
   PZ8.1.H4011ak 2011
   398.2--dc22
   [E]
                                          2010052072

I AM TAMA, LUCKY CAT

A Japanese Legend

Wendy
Henrichs

Illustrated by

Yoshiko
Jaeggi

PEACHTREE
ATLANTA

Many years ago, I was a cat in search of food and shelter.

After a long and tiring journey, I came upon a rundown temple at the foot of a majestic snowcapped mountain.

I sat in the doorway and waited with
my right paw upheld, as is my custom.

The holy man of the temple, a monk
with little more than a few grains of rice
to share, welcomed me in.

I was a lucky cat.

"Little cat," said the monk, "are you hurt?"

I smiled at him with my pale green eyes, for I was not hurt. When I sit, I often raise my paw in the time-honored Japanese greeting, *Come to me!*

"How fortunate to be visited by a Japanese bobtail," he said, "especially one with your rare black and orange coloring. I will name you 'Tama, Lucky Cat' after my boyhood days by the Tama River, where I watched the brilliant, blue-backed kingfishers fly."

My new master had many worries. His temple was falling apart. The roof leaked and there wasn't enough money for firewood.

The few worshippers who came to pray were as poor as he and had no bronze coins for offerings. But my master did not despair. He had learned through Buddha's teachings to be happy in easing the suffering of others.

He never considered his own hunger, but looked with compassion upon the hollow cheeks of his people and the protruding bones beneath my coat.

It was for me and the temple worshippers that he wanted more food...more warmth...more comfort.

He and I often sat together in the overgrown garden of the temple, watching the carp swim between the plum petals floating on the pond.

"Do not worry, Master," I wished to tell him. "I will take care of us. I will bring you good fortune!" But all I could offer was my singsong *mrowww* in a language he could not understand.

Still, he listened to my cat music and loving purrs with great contentment.

Thus far, my gifts to my master were simple: a touch of fur to keep him warm,

a mouse caught to protect our meager rice supply,

and a happy companionship.

These things, though small, were my way of thanking him for all he had given me.

Yes, I was a lucky cat.

The season of cherry blossoms
came and went and came again.

One afternoon, a spring thunderstorm
raged down the mountain. Puddles
formed on the temple's wood floors.

Without warning, I ran out of the
temple and into the mighty storm,
startling my master.

"Tama! Tama!" he cried. "The cold will
be the death of you! Come back,
little cat!"

But I did not go back.

I stopped and sat at the ramshackle temple gate to clean myself.

Lick, rub.
Lick, rub.

In Japan, it is believed that when a cat washes its face, a guest will arrive.

Sure enough, through the pouring rain and blinding flashes, a weary-looking samurai warlord approached on a beautiful white steed. His elegant uniform was soaked, yet he wore it with a fierce dignity.

After one glance at our temple's worn walls and sagging roof, he chose instead to seek shelter beneath the boughs of the blooming cherry tree. Just as the warlord lowered his head to rest, something caught his eye.

Me.

I watched the man and his splendid beast with no fear, no surprise. Pausing from my bath, I raised my paw in welcome.

The warlord stared, a hint of amusement in his face. "Are you beckoning me, Cat?" he asked. He dismounted and took a few steps toward the temple gate.

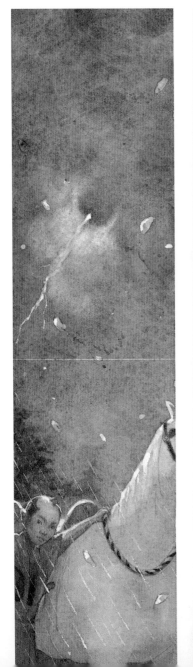

Thunder barreled down the mountain. *BOOM! CLAP! CRASH!*

Closer, closer, the warlord came. Near enough for me to see
raindrops glistening on his brow. And then, as if
Raijin the god of thunder shouted a command
to his lightning demon Raijū...

CRACK!

CREAK!

THUD!

...a staggering bolt struck
the largest bough of the
magnificent cherry tree.

Down the bough fell,
landing heavily in the mud.

The warlord froze, staring
at the spot where he and
his horse had stood just
moments before.

He smiled and knelt before me, humbly bowing his head.

"Thank you, enchanting cat. By bidding me forward, you saved my life. I will come in and make this temple my family's place of honor."

From then on, my master and I wanted for nothing. The warlord, a man of great wealth, restored our temple. No more sagging doorways, no more leaking roofs, and, always, plenty to eat. Our temple walls soon rang with the lively sounds of the warlord's family.

"You truly are a lucky cat," said my master, "for you brought good fortune to us all!"

Each spring, when the cherry trees flower once again, I sit in the grand doorway of our beautiful temple and watch their blossoms dance to the ground. With my paw upheld, I proudly beckon to all who come to worship.

I am Tama, Lucky Cat.

Pagoda on Goutoku-ji Temple grounds

AUTHOR'S NOTE

THE LUCKY CAT LEGEND most likely originated during Japan's early Edo period more than 350 years ago. Although many versions survive, I chose one of the more popular accounts as the basis for I AM TAMA, LUCKY CAT.

According to this version, the Goutoku-ji Temple near Tokyo is where the legendary cat Tama lived and died. Within its grounds, the *Maneki Neko* Beckoning Cat Temple honors Tama with a gravestone and shrine. The cemetery is the burial place for hundreds of other cats. Also buried there are Lord Naotaka Ii, who lived at the beginning of the Edo period, and his family. Many believe him to be the warlord in the legend.

The formal name for Lucky Cat, or Beckoning Cat, is *Maneki Neko. Maneki* means "beckoning" and *Neko* means "cat." Storefront windows and Japanese restaurant counters all around the world display *Maneki Neko*/Lucky Cat figurines, beckoning visitors in with promises of good fortune. Although Lucky Cat figurines come in a variety of colors and styles, the traditional statues share Tama's white, black, and orange coloring.

Lucky Cat figurines

ACKNOWLEDGMENTS

The author, the illustrator, and the publisher would like to thank the following people for their gracious help:

Dr. Melissa Anne-Marie Curley, Assistant Professor of Japanese Religions at the University of Iowa in Iowa City, Iowa; Jerry and Barbara Conner; Mel and Amy Yamano; Seonghee Ryu; Dr. Yukimasa Yamada, Professor of Architectural History at Tokyo Metropolitan University in Tokyo, Japan; and Dr. Mari Nakahara, Reference Librarian, Asian Division, Library of Congress.